L

# Maddie's Millionaire Dreams

Illustrated by Marie-Louise Gay
Translated by Sarah Cummins

**First Novels**

Formac Publishing Company Limited
Halifax
2002

Originally published as *Sophie court après la fortune*
Copyright © 2001 Les éditions de la courte échelle inc
Translation copyright © 2002 Sarah Cummins

Formac Publishing Company Limited acknowledges the support
of the Cultural Affairs Section, Nova Scotia Department of
Tourism and Culture. We acknowledge the financial support of the
Government of Canada through the Book Publishing Industry
Development Program (BPIDP) for our publishing activities.

We acknowledge the support of the Canada Council for the Arts
for our publishing program.

**National Library of Canada Cataloguing in Publication Data**

Leblanc, Louise, 1942-
[Sophie court après la fortune. English]
    Maddie's millionaire dreams / Louise Leblanc;
    illustrated by Marie-Louise Gay.

(First novels ; #44)
Translation of: Sophie court après la fortune.
ISBN 0-88780-579-5 (hdc.).—ISBN 0-88780-578-7 (pbk.)

    I. Gay, Marie-Louise II. Title. III. Title: [Sophie court
    après la fortune. English]. IV. Series.

PS8573.E25S62713 2002        jC843'.54        C2002-903226-1
PZ7

Formac Publishing Company Limited
5502 Atlantic Street
Halifax, Nova Scotia B3H 1G4
www.formac.ca

Printed and bound in Canada

Distributed in the United States by:
Orca Book Publishers
P.O. Box 468 Custer, WA
USA 98240-0468

Distributed in the UK by:
Roundabout Books (a division of
Roundhouse Publishing Ltd.)
31 Oakdale Glen, Harrogate,
N Yorkshire. HG1 2JY

# Table of Contents

# 1
# A Fall from on High

I'm living the life of my dreams. First, I'll have breakfast by the pool, in a tropical garden ringed with palm trees. Afterwards I'll go shopping. There are so many things I'd like to get.

The next thing I know, I'm sitting in my limousine. It's gliding along smoothly, then another car starts honking and honking and honking.

Oh! It was my alarm clock. I squeezed my eyelids shut to keep from waking up. I'm back in my limo.

"Maddie! Are you up?"

The piercing voice of my mother burst the bubble of my dream.

I was back in my bedroom. From my window I could see nothing but three maple leaves. Not a bit like palm trees, I can tell you!

"Maddeeeee!"

I dressed quickly and hurried downstairs. Each step plunged me deeper and deeper into reality. As I entered the kitchen, I was at the deepest point — I'd hit bottom.

"NAAAN!" wailed my little sister, Angelbaby.

That meant "I want my mashed banana right now!" She'd starve to death before she got it, with our dad trying to squash a banana with a spoon. Unbelievable.

My brothers were eating breakfast and quarrelling. Alexander had spread his Tokemon cards out on the table. He was trying to get Julian to buy them, but Julian would have none of it.

"I'll let you have them half price," Alexander wheedled.

"Leave him alone," I advised, putting some bread in the toaster. "He's not interested in your Tokemon."

"But everyone's collecting them!"

"Everyone's stupid. Those cards are hideous."

"They are," Dad agreed. "Anyway, why are you selling them if you're collecting them?"

"So I can buy different ones!"

Poor Alexander. Tokemon has addled his brain.

"Well, you're not buying any more with MY money!" declared Julian.

"You'd rather save your money," Dad said approvingly.

"No, I'd rather spend it on my Tintin collection."

Depressing! My brothers are hopeless consumers, and Dad is incapable of mashing a banana.

"It might work better with a fork," I suggested.

"Good idea," he said, handing me the dish. "I'm going to join your mother and grandmother in the living room."

"Gran's here? I'm coming, too."

But he sat me back down before I could lift as much as an eyebrow.

"No, you stay here! We

grown-ups have to talk. Your grandmother has serious money problems."

"WAAANNNHH!"

Grrrr! I gave Angelbaby a mountain of mashed banana. She shoveled it in, drooling with delight. All it takes is a banana to make Angelbaby happy.

Enjoy it while you can, Angelbaby! Soon enough you'll have money problems like everyone else.

At least at night we can still dream.

"Kids, it's time to get ready to go," my mother said.

I tried to cling to my dream as I climbed into my limo. But then it turned into a pumpkin — a big orange pumpkin of a schoolbus that jerked out onto the road.

I fell back to earth with a thud.

# 2
# Money Worries

It's awfully hard to keep from daydreaming in math class. Ms. Spiegel is soooo boring.

I thought about Gran. I was worried about her. If she had no more money, how would she live? And what about me? Without presents from Gran, I'd sink into poverty.

"Maddie! The answer is...?"

"Uh, one thousand dollars!"

The entire class exploded in guffaws. Except Ms. Spiegel. She didn't laugh. Instead, she multiplied my math homework by two.

At recess my friends
crowded around me, but not
to console me.

"You certainly got your

money's worth," Patrick teased heartlessly.

"Don't count on me to help you," said Clementine, Little Miss Perfect. "I've been swamped ever since I got my computer."

Nicholas said nothing, but only because his mouth was full. All he cares about is emptying his bag of chips. He might at least offer some to me! But he's as selfish as the rest of them.

"When you're in trouble," I muttered despairingly, "you find out who your real friends are."

"Aside from your math problems," sneered Patrick, "what other problems do you have?"

"For your information, since I woke up this morning, I have sunk into poverty."

They were struck dumb. Nicholas even stopped eating. I seized the opportunity to sneak my hand into his bag of chips—but it was empty. Grr!

I told them about my night as a millionaire, my come-down ... and Gran's problems.

"My future looks gloomy."

"Money's not everything, you know," Clementine reminded me in her little mousy voice.

"It's the only thing my parents think about!" Nicholas retorted, opening a package of licorice.

"Without money, you can't do anything," Patrick said.

"You can go to school."
Clementine is so tiresome!

"Yeah, but who wants to go
to school barefoot, on an
empty stomach?" I shot back.

"Do you mean you're so
poor you don't have enough
to eat?" Nicholas was appalled.
He finally offered me a stick
of licorice.

"No," I accepted the licorice.
"I just mean that Clementine
has a full stomach. She can
afford not to care about
money because her parents are
rich."

"Not very rich," Clementine
protested.

"Well, they didn't pay for
your computer with clamshells,
did they?"

Back into your hole,

little mouse!

"You're out of your mind if you expect your parents to give you money," Nicholas declared, stuffing licorice into his mouth.

"But there's a way to get all the money you want," he added, drooling.

Patrick, of course, had to act like he'd heard it all before.

"With a credit card? Forget about it. It's easy enough to get one, but you have to pay afterwards."

Nicholas smiled, showing us all of his blackened teeth.

"No, stupid. Lottery tickets!"

Clementine peeked out of her hole. "Kids aren't allowed to buy lottery tickets."

"Duh!" says Nicholas. "My parents have a corner store!"

"Do you mean you steal them?" Clementine was shocked.

"No, I buy them with the money I earn. Twenty dollars' worth, last week."

We all stared him, transfixed, our eyes as round as quarters.

"If you're interested, I can get you tickets. But you have to pay up front, and I get a double cut of the winnings."

Wow! Nicholas had turned into quite the wheeler-dealer.

But this might be my one and only chance to climb out of poverty.

# 3
# Dream a Little Dream

I had time to think it over during classes and my mind was made up: I wanted to get rich. I decided to accept Nicholas's offer.

Maybe this is the last time I'll do this, I thought as I climbed into the motorized pumpkin they call a school bus.

It started up, scattering us like pumpkin seeds. That shook me from my daydream, and I thought of a serious question: Was there any money in my piggybank?

As soon as the bus stopped,
I hopped off and raced home.
Gran was there! She greeted
us with the announcement that
she had made a sugar pie. My

brothers rushed to the kitchen.

I just wanted to get to my room. But I didn't want to hurt Gran's feelings, so I dutifully ate a piece of pie.

The worst was having to listen to Alexander bragging about his Tokemon cards. He was so proud because he sold one for ten dollars. Wait—

"And I managed to get a card that's incredibly rare!

What a waste! He could have invested his money in my lottery tickets.

"It's not fair," Julian complained. "I can never find any incredibly rare Tintins!"

The two of them were pathetic. I rolled my eyes at Gran but she didn't react. She must be worried about her

money problems.

Hey! There was an idea! I could help Gran by going in with her on the lottery tickets, instead of with Nicholas!

I didn't say anything in front of my brothers. If they joined us, we'd have to split the winnings four ways. But afterwards I would buy them so much Tokemon and Tintin they'd be sick of them.

After they left I helped myself to more pie, and I explained to Gran how we could get out of the dire straits we found ourselves in.

\* \* \*

When I got to my room, I was still reeling.

The long and the short of it was I thought Gran was going to die. She turned every colour of the rainbow and clutched at her heart.

"Never, never the lottery, Maddie! Or any other game of chance! You must run from them like the plague, do you understand?"

What could I do? I promised whatever she asked. But seeing my piggyback reminded me of my ambition to get rich.

It wouldn't be breaking my promise to Gran if I just checked whether there was any money in it.

There was. There was lots. Oh yes, I remembered, I was saving it for Dad's birthday present.

The more I thought it over, the more I felt Gran was over-reacting. She was going through a rough patch. I wouldn't catch the plague just from buying a little scratch-'n-win ticket!

The next day in school, Nicholas made me feel like I was making a smart choice.

"You win every time," he

assured me.

Clementine claimed that wasn't true. But Patrick and I didn't care what she said. We each ordered a ticket from Nicholas.

All day long we planned how we would spend our fortune. By nightfall I was living the life of a millionaire again.

I dreamed I was showing Gran through my magic garden, where money grew on the trees. You just had to shake a branch and the hundred-dollar bills would come floating down.

# 4
# Gambling Fever

The next day Nicholas gave me my lottery ticket. It was like getting a present. I was so excited!

"My heart is beating so fast," I told the others.

"I feel all shivery," Patrick said.

"You guys are sick," commented Clementine.

"It's gambling fever," Nicholas explained. "There's only one cure. When you scratch your ticket, the fever drops."

"But then it goes up again,

like a yo-yo. And you have to get another ticket."

Clementine is such a pain!

"You're falling into a terrible trap," she warned us.

"Oooh, I'm scared," Patrick snickered, gleefully scratching his ticket.

"Well?" asked Nicholas.

"It doesn't say how much I won. It just says *Better luck next time!*"

The next time was me.
I scratched frantically.
I couldn't believe it! *Better luck...* I felt faint with disappointment, as if I had opened a present and found the box was empty.

"No worries, I'll have a winner," Nicholas promised.

You could tell he was used

to it. He made the suspense
last, rubbing his thumb across
the ticket like a snail.

"Come on, Nick!" Patrick
said impatiently.

"This has never happened
before," Nicholas murmured
finally.

"What has never happened before?"

"So much bad luck."

He didn't need to tell us what was written on his ticket.

But Nicholas didn't seem

depressed. He set about boosting our spirits.

"If we try again, there is not one chance in a million that we'll be unlucky again."

He had had so much experience that I felt we could trust him.

So I bought another ticket from him.

* * *

A week later, with a feeling of dread in the pit of my stomach, I prepared to scratch my fifth ticket. I *had* to win this time or I was ruined. My piggybank was empty.

Shiny specks of the coating flew off under my thumbnail, like little stars of hope that flickered and died as I read the words: *Better luck next time.*

I was destroyed. A bomb exploded in my head, an explosion of regret. Followed by an explosion of questions. How could I have been so

crazy? How had I sunk so low?

There was only one answer: I had fallen into the yo-yo trap. It was all Nicholas's fault! His empty promises!

I was about to tell him what I thought when an incredible thing happened. Nicholas started to cry. Through a flood of tears, he confessed that he hadn't had a winning ticket for three weeks!

It was shocking! Had he no shame? You can't get any more rotten than that. I wanted to scratch him out of my life. I only held back because he was already scratched to pieces.

"I never paid for the tickets," he confessed,

sniffling. "In the beginning
my parents just thought there
was a mistake with the cash
register. But not anymore.
Boo hoo! If they ever find out
that I — boohoohoohoo!"

"That's really serious," said
Clementine thoughtfully.

Now she'd give us a lecture, I was sure. But no! Sometimes she can really amaze me!

"Maddie was right," she said. "When you're in trouble, you find out who your real friends are. We have to rescue Nicholas."

Wasn't she forgetting something?

"What about me? I'm ruined! And I can't rescue my Gran, and I can't buy my dad a birthday present, or ..."

"*Whoa!*" Patrick stopped me. "We can't rescue anyone without *money*! There's no way out."

"Why don't we have a rummage sale?" suggested Clementine.

"It takes too long to organize." Nicholas was in a panic. "I have to get the money back in the cash register right away."

"It all depends how much you owe."

"Um, not that much," said Nicholas. "One hundred and twelve dollars."

"Are you out of your mind?" Patrick whistled.

Clementine gulped, "It's worse than I thought!"

Whew, it sure was. Only a miracle could save Nicholas.

# 5
# A Business Plan

Believe it or not, I came up with a plan that will rescue everyone.

And I am more determined than ever to get rich. I never want to fall into debt like Nicholas. It was awful. He was like a fish on a hook, thrashing about in a total panic.

The next morning, he was still twitching nervously. Patrick and Clementine looked like the world was coming to an end. Fortunately I arrived to tell them the good news.

"We're going to start a business and make a fortune. We just need a good product. And the one I have in mind is hot. Kids love it."

They were hanging on to my words, like they hang on to Ms. Spiegel's the day before a test.

"Think," I said. "What could it be?"

"Chips?"

"Don't be an idiot, Nicholas."

"I'm serious," he protested.

Poor Ms. Spiegel. It must be hard to put up with Nicholas sometimes.

"Come on, spit it out, Maddie."

She must have the patience of a saint, to endure Patrick!

"It's obvious—Tokemon cards! Little kids are crazy about them. It's worse than lottery tickets. Alexander wastes all his money on them."

"You're forgetting one thing," Patrick reminded me. "Before we can sell them, we have to buy them."

"No, we don't!" cried Nicholas. "I'll just take them from the store."

"What have you got for brains, Nicholas? Licorice?" Clementine was angry. "You're already in the hole for $112! Isn't that enough?"

"*Quiet*! Are you guys going to listen to me?"

Honestly, there are limits to one's patience!

"With my plan, all we need is certain *rare* cards. They're worth their weight in gold. We don't need to buy them; we only need to borrow them, because we are going to *print* them."

They looked at me in stupefaction, then they all began talking at once.

"That is a genius plan," Patrick exclaimed.

"I'm not so sure," murmured Clementine.

"If I could get a word in edgewise," said Nicholas, "I might mention that there is a photocopier in the st—"

"No," I cut him off. "For professional quality work, the best thing to do is to use Clementine's computer."

Before she could refuse, I asked her if she still wanted to help her friends who were in trouble.

"Yes, of course," she squeaked, like a mouse caught in a trap.

I know I put her on the spot, but when you're starting a business, you can't worry about everybody's feelings all the time.

"Okay, here's what we do. By tomorrow, each of you has to come up with a rare card."

"If I've got this straight, I can't get it from the store, right?" Nicholas fretted.

"How are we supposed to get rare cards without any money?" Patrick asked.

"Um, I think I already have what we need," announced Clementine, blushing.

She revealed that she already had an extensive collection of Tokemon cards.

"I was younger then," she said defensively. "I haven't bought any for ages."

"So you walked into the trap like everyone else," mocked Patrick.

He is such a bumbler. Now
was not the time to offend
Little Miss Perfect, not when
we needed her help.

"I can't believe it! You of
all people!" he kept on. I had
to stop him.

"Well, Patrick, you collect
hockey cards."

"Right," Nicholas pitched in. "Anyway, the important thing is to rescue me as quickly as possible."

With no candy to munch on, he began attacking his last remaining fingernail. He didn't dare take anything from the store anymore.

"Okay!" I said. "That means we can start printing today after school. This evening I'll test our product on Alexander. And tomorrow we can begin selling."

Boy, were they impressed. It seemed like a good time to tell them about my decision.

"After Nicholas's debt is paid off, I'm taking a double cut of the profits."

Business is business, after all!

"What is the reason for that?" demanded Clementine.

"It was my idea, and I organized it all!"

"Well, I'm contributing the computer and the cards. I deserve just as big a share. And if I don't get it ..."

I couldn't believe it! I had to give in, but I told her what I thought.

"Honestly, Clementine, I would never have thought it of you!"

She made a miserable little face.

"I'm fed up with waiting for my parents to give me money. I need my own money. You should understand that!"

I did understand one thing perfectly. She was just like all rich people. The more they have, the more they want. They're so greedy!

# 6
# Lose Some, Win Some

I had to admit that Little Miss Perfect did a good job. That very evening I showed my brothers the Tokemon cards, hot off the press.

"This is Clementine's collection. I thought you might be interested, Alexander."

"I don't know," he said. "I don't buy just anything."

He examined the cards.

"That's strange," he said, shaking his head. My heart lurched.

"What? What's strange?"

"This is a card I've never seen before."

Whew! Easy enough to explain that.

"That's because these are very *rare* cards."

"How come Clementine has so many of them?" asked Julian.

"Uh, because they're old cards!"

"How come they look so new?" the little genius kept on.

I gulped, but no explanation came to me. I was engulfed in counterfeiter's panic—the fear of discovery.

"Because Clementine is a collector who takes good care of her collection," Alexander explained to him.

Saved! And by the victim himself! I had nothing to worry about.

The next morning I was able to reassure the others.

"Alexander didn't suspect a thing!"

They were euphoric! I had a super-motivated sales team! I handed out the cards and sent them into the schoolyard.

We regrouped a little while

later to touch base. Nobody had expressed any suspicion, and we had made total sales of sixteen dollars.

"Not bad," said Clementine appreciatively.

"Not enough to pay off my debts," said Nicholas, still worried. "I'm really in hot water at the store."

"At this rate, I'll never see any cash," grumbled Patrick.

"What are you insinuating?" demanded Clementine.

"Everyone gets their cut before me! I want my share now!"

A brawl broke out. They were like dogs fighting over a bone. They were so disappointing!

I tried to restore harmony.

"If you guys weren't so

pathetic, we could all make a
pile."

At least they stopped
squabbling long enough to
listen to me.

"I think the cards have been

tested enough. Now we take them to a bigger market. We'll flood the market, and the money will come pouring in."

"It's too risky!" Clementine shuddered.

"If you're afraid to swim, stay in the bathtub," Patrick sneered.

I told the little mouse the straight truth.

"If you want to succeed, you have to be ambitious! Don't you want to be independent of your parents?"

"Ye-es," she finally admitted.

"There are two card stores near the school," I pushed my advantage. "We'll take turns going there. And everyone can keep a share of the earnings. How's that?"

They all agreed we would start that day. At least they agreed on something.

* * *

At lunchtime my plan was put into action.

And afterwards we all met up again in the principal's office.

The upshot was that the store owners accused us of fraud. They discovered our scam by asking us the same questions that Julian had. But unlike Julian, they weren't satisfied with the answers.

The other kids all panicked and blamed everything on me.

Cowards! Rats always abandon a sinking ship. They were all willing to take the profits but not the risk. They were as guilty as I was!

I wasn't going down without defending myself, so I revealed the real reason for our business: to pay off Nicholas's lottery debts.

My friends all looked at me as if I were a traitor. That was the last straw. I burst into tears.

* * *

In the end, we were all rescued by our parents. Well, that's one way of looking at it. In my case, the consequences were terrible. I lost everything — my money, my friends, my brothers.

Alexander was pitiless.

"I never want to speak to

you again," he told me.

"Me neither," said Julian.
"You might sell me counterfeit
Tintin books."

Even my mother and father rejected me. They went out to the movies so they wouldn't have to be with me.

I was left all alone with my despair.

"Do you want to tell me about it, honey?"

It was Gran! I threw myself into her arms and cried my heart out. When I felt calmer, I told her everything. I made sure she knew one thing.

"The main reason I wanted to get rich was to rescue you!"

And then I got a big surprise. Gran informed me that she wasn't in financial ruins. But her brother was, and for the same reason as me.

"He gambled everything away at the casino. He wrote bad cheques to pay off his debts, and he was arrested for fraud. He thought that gambling was a quick and easy way to get rich, just like you did."

"But everyone dreams of being rich, Gran! What's wrong with that?"

"It's all right to want to have money, Maddie. But not so much that you'd do anything to get it! You shouldn't let it turn into an obsession. Money's not everything."

Her words reminded me of Little Miss Perfect and the other kids in my gang.

"Wherever there's money, there's fighting over money. None of my friends are even speaking to me," I said.

"You could write them a letter and tell them you want to talk to them about what happened," Gran suggested.

Listening to Gran, I got a brilliant idea.

I should write a book about my experience. It would help others to avoid the trap that I fell into. I'm sure my book would be wildly successful, and I would make lots of money!

Then I wouldn't have to chase after money ever again. Whew!

# Three more new novels in the *First Novels Series*!

## Dear Old Dumpling
*By Gilles Gauthier*

Dumpling is very young, just having celebrated his first birthday, and he needs some help growing up. Carl's mother thinks he might be in love, so the boys and their dog set off around the neighbourhood so that young Dumpling can find his true love!

## Fred's Halloween Adventure
*Marie-Danielle Croteau*

Fred is going to spend Halloween with his friend William and they are going to be part of the pumpkin festival. Fred finds he has agreed to be Cinderella and travel inside a huge pumpkin — a trip that turns into a disaster.

## Marilou Cries Wolf
*By Raymond Plante*

Marilou is bored so she plays a trick on Boris and then another one on the twins. No one is amused. So they play a trick on Marilou so that she will never, ever cry wolf again.

---

**Formac Publishing Company Limited**
5502 Atlantic Street, Halifax, Nova Scotia B3H 1G4
Orders: 1-800-565-1975 Fax: (902) 425-0166
www.formac.ca